PIÑATA PARTY

by Martha E. Kendall

illustrated by Unada

Author Martha E. Kendall, a professor of English and Women's Studies at San Jose City College in California, is the recipient of several awards for excellence in teaching and in 1986 was honored at the National Women's Hall of Fame.

To Jeff and Katie
I hope you have many happy piñata parties.

Published by Worthington Press
801 94th Avenue North, St. Petersburg, Florida 33702

Copyright © 1993 by Worthington Press

Printed in the United States of America

2 4 6 8 10 9 7 5 3 1

ISBN 0-87406-654-9

Julie and her twin brother Joshua were having trouble agreeing on something important.

Julie said, "For our birthday, I want to have a fairy tale party. We can all dress up as our favorite characters. I'll be Cinderella."

4

"Yuck!" said Joshua. "I want to have a dinosaur party. And I'll be Tyrannosaurus Rex."

"Yuck!" said Julie.

Then their friend Antonio had an idea. "How about a fiesta?" he asked.

"You mean we all take a nap? No way!" the twins answered at the same time.

"No," said Antonio. "Not a *siesta*. A *fiesta!* That's a Mexican party. We could even make a piñata!"

"Yes, yes!" Julie and Joshua shouted.

But then Joshua asked, "What is a piñata?"

"Is it something you put pins in?" Julie asked.

Antonio smiled and said, "A piñata is a paper animal filled with surprises. At parties, kids take turns hitting it with a broom handle until it breaks. Then out come toys and candies for everybody! Let's go inside. I'll help you make one."

Antonio blew up a big balloon.

He told Julie how to make paste from flour and water.

Then Antonio said to Joshua, "Tear some newspaper into strips."

Joshua tore a few pieces, but he was slow because he kept stopping to look at the comics in the newspaper.

Antonio said, "Try to go a little faster, Joshua. We still have to dip the newspaper strips into the paste and press them onto the balloon. I'll help you."

The boys tore and tore, and soon they had enough pieces. Then the three friends covered the balloon with them.

After letting the piñata dry overnight, the friends
got together again. Antonio carefully made a small
hole in the piñata.

"What are you doing?" Julie cried. "Don't put a hole
in our brand new piñata!"

Antonio explained, "That's a hole for putting the
candy and toys inside the piñata."

"Oh," said Julie. "Then make the hole even bigger!"

So they did. When they were finished, they painted
the piñata with bright colors.

"*I* want it to be a donkey," said Julie. She cut out big gray ears from construction paper. Then she glued the ears to the piñata.

"*I* want it to be an elephant," said Joshua. He cut out a long elephant's trunk from construction paper. Then he glued the trunk to the piñata.

Antonio said to his friends, "Amigos, how about if we make it an iguana?"

"What's that?" Julie and Joshua asked.

"It's a special kind of lizard," Antonio said. "There are a lot of them in Mexico." He glued a long streamer onto the piñata. "Now the piñata has an iguana tail," he said.

Then Antonio laughed and chased Julie and Joshua around the kitchen, sticking his tongue in and out like a lizard.

On the day of Julie and Joshua's birthday party,
their friends did not know what to expect when
Antonio brought in a broom. Some of the kids acted a
little scared. Some of them laughed excitedly.

"What does this mean?" one boy asked.

"You'll find out in just a minute!" said Julie.

Next, Antonio carried in the piñata. It looked heavy.
He got some help from Julie and Joshua's dad, who
tied it up high.

Antonio explained what to do. The kids took turns hitting the piñata with the end of the broom.

They hit the piñata harder and harder. The piñata's donkey ears jiggled. Its elephant trunk and iguana tail wiggled. The boys and girls giggled.

Finally, Julie whacked the piñata so hard it cracked. Then Joshua hit it again and. . .CRASH! The piñata opened up, and all the surprises tumbled out.

Soon, the floor was covered with surprises! Everybody scrambled to get the marbles, little astronauts, silver-colored rings, race cars, tops, tiny dolls, sheriff's badges, butterscotch candies, and chocolates.

Next it was time for cake.

"*I* want to blow out the candles," said Joshua.

"*I* want to blow out the candles," said Julie.

Antonio said to his friends, "Don't worry, amigos."
He set the cake between them, and they both blew out
the candles.

Then the twins began to open all the presents their friends had brought. Antonio smiled when they got to the gifts from him.

"That's my present to you–Mexican sombreros," he said.

It was the best birthday party ever.

As Antonio and the rest of their friends were leaving, Julie and Joshua told them goodbye and thank you: "Adios! Gracias!" they said.

The twins felt very tired. Now that the fiesta was over, they were ready for a siesta! And before they knew it, they were sound asleep, dreaming about their piñata party.

How To Make A Piñata

Making a piñata is fun and easy. Just follow the steps on this page. When you're done, get a grown-up to help you hang up the piñata. Then have fun hitting it until it breaks open!

What you need:

- a big balloon, blown up
- paste (either wallpaper paste OR 1 cup of flour mixed with 1 cup of water OR 1 cup of white glue mixed with 1 cup of water)
- lots of newspaper strips, 1 to 2 inches wide and 5 to 10 inches long
- blunt-nosed scissors
- paints and brushes
- a wire coat hanger
- candy and small toys

What to do:

1. Dip the newspaper strips into the paste. Press them onto the balloon. Overlap the strips, and make several layers. Let the piñata dry overnight.

2. Paint the piñata. (You can also draw on it with markers. If you want to get even more fancy, glue crepe paper streamers or shapes cut from construction paper onto the piñata.)

3. Cut a small, banana-shaped slit at the top of the piñata. Open the slit just enough to push toys and candy inside.

4. With a grown-up helping, bend the hanger until it is straight, with the handle at the top. Push all but the handle through the slit and into the piñata. The handle will be the hook for carrying or hanging the piñata.